The Berenstain Bears
AND TOO MUCH
Teasing

"He's her own brother,
but Sister is pleased
when the tables are turned
and Brother gets teased.

A FIRST TIME BOOK®

Teasing

Stan & Jan Berenstain

Random House New York

Copyright © 1995 by Berenstain Enterprises, Inc. All rights reserved under International and Pan-American Copyright Conventions. Published in the United States by Random House, Inc., New York, and simultaneously in Canada by Random House of Canada Limited, Toronto.
Library of Congress Cataloging-in-Publication Data
Berenstain, Stan The Berenstain Bears and too much teasing / Stan & Jan Berenstain.
   p.   cm. — (First time books)   SUMMARY: Brother Bear likes to tease his sister, but when he's the one who is taunted at school, he understands why Sister gets so mad.   ISBN: 0-679-87706-1 (pbk.) — 0-679-97706-6 (lib. bdg.)
[1. Behavior—Fiction. 2. Conduct of life—Fiction. 3. Schools—Fiction. 4. Bears—Fiction. 5. Brothers and sisters—Fiction.] I. Berenstain, Jan. II. Title. III. Series: Berenstain, Stan. First time books.
PZ7.B4483Beltj 1995 [E]—dc20 95-1634
Manufactured in the United States of America
10 9 8 7 6 5 4 3 2 1

Brother and Sister Bear agreed about the important things in life. They agreed that Christmas and Halloween were the two best holidays.

They agreed that no school was better than school.
They agreed that sweet potatoes were better than
mashed potatoes.

But there were some things they didn't agree on.

Brother's favorite colors were red and blue. Sister's favorite colors were pink and more pink.

Brother's favorite ice cream flavor was chocolate. Sister's was pistachio.

Brother liked spooky movies. Sister hated spooky movies.

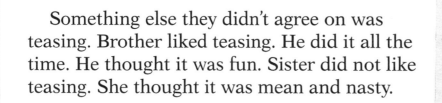

Something else they didn't agree on was teasing. Brother liked teasing. He did it all the time. He thought it was fun. Sister did not like teasing. She thought it was mean and nasty.

Mama talked to Brother about teasing and how it wasn't such a good idea. She talked to Sister about not being so sensitive.

Papa thought that too much fuss was being made about it all. "Teasing is just part of life. Isn't that right, Ookums Snookums?" he said, tickling Mama under the chin.

"You know I don't like to be called that," said Mama. "*Nor* do I like to be tickled under the chin!"

Brother Bear found out that both Mama and Papa were right. Teasing wasn't such a good idea, and it *was* part of life. He found it out in a way he did not enjoy.

One day at Bear Country School something a little unusual happened.

"Mr. Honeycomb wants to see you in his office, Brother Bear," his teacher said. The class was abuzz. What had Brother done? Why did Mr. Honeycomb, the principal, want to see Brother in his office? Brother Bear was worried. But he needn't have been.

"Brother Bear," said Mr. Honeycomb, "I need a special messenger to carry messages to the different classrooms. Both your marks and your behavior have been excellent. I have chosen you to be my special messenger. Report to me at the start of school each day, and I will give you the messages you are to deliver. You may go back to class now."

As you might guess, word about Brother's special job got around fast. Many cubs were a little jealous of Brother. Some cubs were a lot jealous. Too-Tall Grizzly and his gang were the most jealous. It wasn't long before Brother Bear, the teaser, began to get teased.

He got teased in class.

He got teased in the schoolyard.

He got teased on the school bus.

He didn't like it. He didn't like it one bit.
"Now *you* know what it's like to get teased,"
said Sister.

Brother didn't say
anything. There wasn't much
he *could* say. All the things
that Brother, the teaser, had
said about teasing were now
being said to him.

He got so angry that he was almost going to fight Too-Tall and his gang, even though they were bigger than he was. But if he did that, he would lose his special job, and just be in worse trouble.

"Oooh!" he said one morning. "I have a stomach ache! I don't think I can go to school today."

"Perhaps you have the 24-hour virus," said Mama. "Sister, will you please get the thermometer?"

"Yes, Mama," said Sister. "But I don't think Brother has the 24-hour virus, or the 48-hour virus, or the 72-hour virus. I think what Brother has is the teasing virus."

"Hmm," said Mama, taking the thermometer from his mouth. "Temperature's normal. Finish your breakfast, cubs. The school bus will be here any minute."

As the bus got closer and closer to the
school, Brother got more and more worried.
He knew exactly what was waiting for him.

Too-Tall and the gang
would tease him in the hall,
in the auditorium,

and in the lunchroom.

But he was wrong. He was wrong because something wonderful had happened!

There was a new cub at Bear Country School. A big, oversize cub with hay in his fur and big, baggy overalls with patches. His name was Milton Chubb. He wore little, round glasses and a little smile on his big, round face. Wow, thought Brother, what a relief! Too-Tall and his gang were looking at Milton the way a wolf looks at a plump chicken.

Brother just knew they would tease the new cub. If they did, he thought, maybe—just maybe—they'll forget about teasing me. That's exactly what happened. They teased Milton on the soccer field when he kicked the ball into the wrong goal and scored for the other side.

They teased him on the baseball field when he missed a fly ball.

They teased him on the basketball court when he dribbled the ball off his foot.

"Hey, Milton," said Too-Tall. "What *is* your game? Is it tiddlywinks? Or hopscotch? Or…" That's when Brother Bear forgot about being happy that he wasn't the one being teased. He stuck up for the new cub.

"Too-Tall," he said, "why don't you let him alone? He's not bothering you!"

"Well, lah-di-dah!" said Too-Tall. "The principal's pet is sticking up for Massive Milton!"

"Come on, Milton," said Brother. "Let's get away from these teasers. Where do you live?"

"On Farmer Ben's farm," he said. "My mom and dad are Farmer Ben's new hired bears."

"Hey," said Brother, "that means we're neighbors. I live in the big tree house just down the road."

That day after school, Brother and Sister Bear visited Milton on Farmer Ben's farm. Milton may not have known much about soccer, baseball, and basketball, but he knew quite a bit about farming.

He was very good at pitching hay (that's why he always had some in his fur).

He was such a good milker that he could
squirt some milk right into the barn cat's mouth.

And he knew how to feed a
sugar cube to a horse without
getting his fingers bitten.

"Milton," said Brother, "you don't play soccer, baseball, or basketball. What *is* your game?"

"Rasslin'!" said Milton.

"Rasslin'?" said Sister. "Oh, you mean wrestling."

Just then, one of Farmer Ben's pigs got out of the pigpen.

"Excuse me," said Milton.

The pig never had a chance. Milton just sort of fell on him. Then he wrestled him back into the pen.

Hmm, thought Brother.

The next morning, the principal's special messenger took a message to the gym and gave it to the coach— but the message wasn't from the principal. "Hmm," said the coach when he read it.

When the cubs came to gym class later that day, they were surprised to see that Milton was already there. He was dressed in wrestling tights, and the coach held several more pairs.

"Cubs," announced the coach. "We are going to organize a wrestling team. Perhaps later we will join the Bear Country Inter-Scholastic Wrestling League. Too-Tall, you and the gang get into these tights. Let's see what you can do against Milton.

"Do you have a favorite hold, Milton?" he asked while Too-Tall and the gang got ready.

"Yes," said Milton. "It's called The Pancake."

"Ready...*wrestle!*" said the coach. Too-Tall came at Milton fast and low. But it really didn't matter. Milton just sort of fell on him.

"Oof!" said Too-Tall. Milton made short work of the rest of the gang, too. There were three Pancakes, followed by three "Oofs!"

Bear Country School joined the wrestling league. The team did pretty well—especially Milton, who won all his matches. Brother and Sister came to all the matches and led the cheering.

Brother and Sister still agree about the important things in life—things like holidays, school, and potatoes. But now there is one thing more they agree about—teasing. They agree that it is still part of life, but it really isn't a very good idea.